THE FISH ⊥   ЗAUCE
INC⌐   ⊥

For W.

THE FISH IN WHITE SAUCE INCIDENT

STORIES BY

JACKIE HODGMAN

KMP

First published 1992
ISBN 1 870978 47 1

Keith Murray Publishing
46 Portal Crescent
Tillydrone
Aberdeen AB2 2SP
© Jackie Hodgman 1992

ACKNOWLEDGEMENTS

Cover design and cover illustrations by Scott Paton

Typeset from disc, prepared by Maggie Seaton,
by Books Unlimited (Nottm)

Printed & bound by Waverley Press (Aberdeen) Ltd

CONTENTS

The Fish In White Sauce Incident

The number of times I've imagined this. Wished for it. Dreamt of it. Now it's happened I can't believe it. It's an anti-climax. Like everything, I suppose. You imagine, anticipate, hope and when it comes ... puff! up go your dreams in smoke.

I'm trying to remember the first thing I remember about you. Bigness, I think. Being held and squeezed, squashed, trapped, imprisoned, restricted. Yes, that's it, restricted. That's the very word.

You're so pathetic now, so small. I can't believe now, now that I look at you, that you were so easy to hate. So intimidating. So bullying. Yes, I like that word. Bullying. I'm trying to imagine what you would have said if I had told you all those years ago that you were nothing but a bully.

"Me!" you would say, "me!" And you would have that tone in your voice. That tone which was like Shakespeare's prose, so dense with meaning. The tone which said, "You don't know what you are talking about. You live in cloud cuckoo land. Me, I'm the one that knows. I know *you*. You don't know nothing. Bullying. I'll tell you what it's like. You don't know how lucky you are. You've had it easy. I'm the one. Not you. ME!"

And of course in the process of defending yourself against the charge you would do what you did every day of my life. You would attack me. Make me feel guilty because I had it easy. I didn't know what the world was about. And then after the guilt, the threat. "One day," you would say, "one day! You'll find out what the world is all about. What will you do

1

then? Eh? Eh? Eh? I hope I'm not around to see that. I'll be the one who has to pick up the pieces. I'm the one. I'm always the one."

Aye, you're always the one, all right. The one who's always there to pick up the pieces? Is that what you think? Oh, you're the one, all right. The one to smash everything up. The one to ruin everything. The accuser. The bloody martyr, that's what you are, always the bloody martyr.

Bullying? No, not you! Do you know this? I can't remember a single day's happiness I had with you. I can't think of a minute's happiness because of you. Oh, but wait a minute. You would say that ALL my happiness was because of you. I suppose that's what you would say. But no happiness was ever caused by you.

I remember a time ... ah, what's the use ... if I told you, you would deny it. I would be wrong. Your subjective memory would come into play and I would be guilty again. It would be all my fault.

Of course it was different with HER. She wasn't wrong. There was always extenuating circumstances for HER.

Christ, how I hated her! How I hated you! You were evil and vindictive. You saw weakness and attacked. "Me? Me? I was evil? How can I have been evil. I did everything for you," you would say. Don't give me this ME shit. But I forget. That's all I ever got from you was ME ME ME ME – always bloody Me. Have you ever? ... did you ever ... think of anyone apart from yourself in this whole goddamned world? Once? Even once?

I can laugh about it now, but for a long time ... for a long time I would have happily killed you. I could, quite easily, have choked the life out of you. I wouldn't even have shot you. Nothing remote like poisoning or shooting. I would have got my hands round your miserable throat and choked the very breath out of your fat, pudgy body. And laughed.

Why? Why didn't you like me? What did I do wrong? I liked you. Loved you. Till you started torturing me. Till you turned me inside out. Do you remember you used to do that to my socks? Turn them half inside out so they looked like wee, backless slippers. You turned me into a wee, backless thing as well.

2

Why? Why? Why did you do it? Why did you hate me so much? Were you jealous? Was that it? Were you frightened of what you had made? Why so much pain?

You never laid a hand on me, I know. But there are more ways of hurting someone than with a backhander. Verbal abuse, emotional withdrawal, constant, constant, constant criticism. That's really backhanded.

Do you remember? Ach, what's the point? You never listen. Not once in my whole life have you listened to me without waiting for a gap, a pause, just long enough for you to interject. Pull yourself up to your full height, what was it, five one, two? and say in that tone, the tone that indicates finality, authority, infinity: "The thing is ..." and no matter what I had been saying, you would then pronounce. That was the law. There was no arguing ... well that's not strictly true; I could go on to argue till the cows come home but if I did, the other tone would come in. The little laugh. "Oh well, if that's what you think," you would say. The mocking tone, the tone which says I'm being very tolerant in listening to you, even though I know you're wrong.

But no. Why the hell should I? I'm going to have my say. Finally. Listen. Just once listen to me. For once in your life stop thinking about yourself. Stop being right. Contemplate the fact that there are other people in the world. Listen to ME.

Do you remember the fish in white sauce? I know it was years ago, but I don't see that that matters. A trivial incident maybe? But if it was so bloody trivial, how come I remember it so clearly. The fish in white sauce incident. I'm sorry but I'm not going to let you off the hook. Get it?

I had made the fish in white sauce, I had friends in, we all ate it. Everyone liked it. Except you. What was it you said again? Can't remember? Don't worry, I can. "Was it no a wee bit thingmy?" For someone so inarticulate you can certainly make your point.

"Thingmy" could, I suppose, mean anything, but there was very little doubt that what you meant was not good. The look of shock on the faces of my friends. My embarrassment. Neither made you stop, think, consider that it might be unkind, rude, ungracious? No, not you! Someone leaped to my defence. Of course, that made it worse. Stated the obvious. If everyone had ignored you. But no. Now it was out in the open. Everyone knew what was happening.

"It was lovely," someone said. "Ha, ha," you said. "Just one of my wee jokes."

No one laughed.

"She knows me," you said. "She knows my sense of humour." Know you? By God, I knew you. But by God, I wish I didn't.

The funny thing was, of course, you liked the meal. You just like to pretend. To upset people. There has never been a meal ever that you have not implied that you don't like. "Oh, it was lovely," you'd say. But you'd say it in a way that suggested you didn't find it lovely at all, but were just trying to be polite. Of course, you were never trying to be polite, but trying, and I hasten to add, succeeding, in making your dislike obvious.

But, of course, it's all a bluff within a bluff. You liked it, the meal, and said so, but in such a way as to make it appear as if you didn't really and were only saying so. Yes, it all works like a charm. You can't be faulted.

Are you wondering why I waited until now to tell you all this. Are you thinking to yourself, "Why didn't she say something earlier? Why wait thirty years? Why put up with thirty years of misery – of bottling up feelings?" Are you wondering?

Well I'll tell you. First, of course, I was intimidated by you. Which, if you think about it, is hardly surprising, if you consider the way our conversations used to run. You ranting, me trying to speak, you interrupting if I did manage to say anything, which was most unusual. I remember once spending ten minutes trying to say one sentence; every time I opened my mouth you would lunge in with your opinion. By the time I finally got to speak I was so upset I burst into tears and gabbled meaningless rubbish. Whatever I said would be treated with total contempt so it didn't really matter either way.

But then afterwards ... as I got to know you I began to pity you.

Yes, pity. You were bloody pathetic, like all bullies. After a while you annoyed me, irritated me, sometimes enraged me, very often frustrated me but never again intimidated.

Do you know what I hated most? Let me give you some examples.

It's funny, there are hundreds of things I could think of. But right now all I keep getting is that image of you in the hospital. Small and frail in a hospital gown. Old and looking up at the young doctor like a child. "It's all right," I kept saying. "Don't worry," I kept saying.

"Let's have you up on the couch," the doctor said. And you looked at me like a frightened, timid, cowed animal.

That's when I realised the futility of it all. That's when I realised that all those years of pain were for nothing. It wasn't that you hated me, it was just that you were frightened, you were frightened so like a cornered animal you hit out. Oh, you hated me all right but you hated yourself as much, in fact you hated the whole world. Everybody in it and being in it yourself. You had a huge personal vendetta against the world but the world was big and frightening and out of reach so you took it out on me. By the time I realised this it was too late. You had made monsters out of both of us.

That's the door. That'll be them now. Long? No, they are never long in these incidents. Come in, officer. Yes, she's in there. I phoned. Yes, that's right, I'm the daughter. Doctor? No, I didn't bother with a doctor. Too late for a doctor. Calm? Yes, I suppose I am calm. Mercy killing? In a way I think it was. Mercy for me, anyway. Och, no, that's not fair. Mercy for you too, eh, Mum? Not only have I escaped from the hellhole you imprisoned me in but I've relieved you of the responsibility of being my jailer.

The Price of Trainers

He used to be a teacher. I think. That would certainly explain a lot. Like where he got the belt from. The tawse. The Lochgelly. Funny, when I was at school no-one ever called it the tawse or the Lochgelly, it was just the belt. Anyway. That would explain where it came from.

"You've been a naughty girl," he would say in a teacherly tone. "And you know what happens to naughty girls. Don't you?"

At this point in the routine I nod sheepishly. He is not satisfied with that.

"Don't you?" he says again.

"Yes," I say at this point.

"What happens to naughty girls?"

"They get their bottoms sp..."

Oh, shite. I've cocked it up again. I don't know how I managed to get it wrong. It's not as if I have a lot of lines to learn. "They get their pants taken down," I say.

"And?" he says.

"They get their bottoms spanked," I say.

It's like a pantomime really. You know the way they say "Oh, yes it is" and we all shout back "Oh, no it isn't".

At this point he produces the Lochgelly. It's under his jacket, hanging over his shoulder. He brings it out and holds it up. It's so hard and thick that it stands up. He holds the wee handle bit at the bottom and it's erect except for the two wee forked bits at the top, they droop slightly. It's amazing, you know, someone invented that. Actually sat down and worked out the best implement for battering weans with. The handle, for easier wielding, the forked bits to lick up your wrists and leave red weals. Sadist. Pervert. So he's standing there with this big black, hard, erect thing in his hand. At this point I give a slight whimper.

"No!" I plead, but of course it's no use.

"Bend over," he says.

Now by this time I know he means over the leather Chesterfield couch. So I do it. He comes up behind me and lifts up my gym slip. I never wore a gym slip in my life before. Funny old world. The surprising thing is – well it's not surprising any more – but the first time it was, he's so gentle. Almost tenderly, he lifts the hem and tucks it into my belt, well, it's not a belt, really, it's a sort of sash thing. He provides the outfit. I wouldn't have a clue where to buy a bloody gym slip. Then he takes down the navy knickers to my knees, exactly at my knees they have to sit. Almost lovingly, he brushes his hand over my backside, just touching me and no more.

He makes a wee speech then. I always feel a bit daft at this bit. I sometimes imagine what would happen if someone happened to look in the window or something. I would look such a eejit with my bare bum in the air and him speechifying. He tells me it will hurt him more than it will hurt me etc. Warns me against making a racket or squirming or anything. All very ritualistic. Then I hear the belt tap against the back of his shoulders. Then I hear the swish it makes flying through the air. WHACK. The pain of the first stroke is always the worst but I tell myself that it will be over soon. And I think of the money. Thirty quid is not bad. It works out at a fiver a stroke. I think of the fiver. The weans need shoes and Donna wants these bloody trainers. I'll be lucky if I can get trainers for thirty quid. Six of the belt later and I'm duly chastised.

There is absolutely no doubt about it, my arse is killing me but it's all over in about ten minutes. That's not a bad rate of pay. Probably more than pilots get.

When the ritual flogging is over, he excuses himself. I lift the three tenners off the table, put my jeans back on and let myself out. I don't see him afterwards. Until the next time. Same time, same place.

I've often wondered what he gets out of it. Does he come while he's doing it, or does he barge off to the bathroom afterwards and masturbate like a fiend? Is it the power that turns him on? He's a queer bird. Always the same suit, three piece, grey, old as the hills. A white shirt, maroon tie. He must be worth a few bob. Apart from the thirty quid a week to me, the house is pretty posh. Nice area, antiques, that sort of thing. Not that I've seen it all, of course, just the hall and "the headmaster's study" as he calls it. There is an atmosphere like a church, quiet and undisturbed, a mothbally, fusty smell. Big, dark, polished furniture, stained glass windows, sort of unlived-in feel. I wonder if he has, or ever had, a wife. I wonder if he ever belted her bum. Doubt it.

When I'm letting myself out I tiptoe through the big old hall, not making a noise as if I would disturb something. I don't know why I do this, but I always do.

Outside it is bright and sunny. Usually I go straight home. On the bus, past the university, the art galleries, past the Victorian terraces, the wally closes, down by the renovated tenements, then past the boarded-up shops, into the scheme, the grafitti on the walls, the groups of neds hanging about the corners, the high rise flats, the three ups with the verandahs with washing hanging up, or piled high with junk. Then up the stairs with the dogs barking. Into the house with the telly blaring. The weans fighting. Donna moaning about Gerry and Gerry complaining about being starving.

But not today. Today I'm looking for trainers, Not buying today. Just looking, trying to find a pair I can afford so that when Donna and I come into town I can direct her to a reasonably cheap pair, by that I mean less than thirty quid. If I don't, it's odds on she'll spot a pair about fifty quid.

I stand at the bus stop and suddenly it strikes me as funny. I look at the people and wonder what they would think about my occupation. Here I stand an ordinary wee wumman. Arse tanned rid raw fur money. "Hoor," I dare say they would say. So what? It's a living. Supplements the supplementary.

I'm going to get something nice for the tea tonight. Chops maybe. Make a nice change from sausages. The weans would like that. I'm walking past a building site when one of the workers hangs off the scaffolding and whistles at me.

"Hello darlin'," he shouts.

He's got the low slung denims on. Slung under his beer belly, two sizes too big for him. Probably showing half his bahookie as well. He doesn't turn round, so I just assume that bit.

"Howz yer bum fur lovebites, hen?" he shouts.

Lovebites, pal! You don't know the half of it.

The Nights Are Fair Drawing In

It had seemed like a good idea at the time. Well, don't they all, right enough? But now Ruth was beginning to have second thoughts. It was dark. Really dark and raining and cold and they were lost. John peered out through the windscreen, the road serpentined before them, each bend visible only seconds before it was upon them. The road like a corkscrew, a part of the country entirely new to them, a black dismal dreich night. It was a great beginning to a holiday. She looked at the map. It was pretty useless – apart from anything else she was rotten at map reading and there was no light to see by anyway. If she turned on the light in the car she could just about make it out – but then the glare prevented John from driving.

At the time, in the middle of a bright September afternoon it had seemed a wonderful idea. A week long break in a farm cottage in the borders. Lovely. Neither of them had been there before; the cottage sounded wonderful. "Off The Beaten Track" the advert had said. How true! Off the bloody map as well. They had been driving down one track roads for hours. Going round and round in circles, no doubt. What on earth possessed them to come straight from work. Why didn't they wait until Saturday morning?

Too late now. Anyway, they probably couldn't even find their way home now. Nothing for it but to persevere.

Suddenly, Ruth screamed. "Look! A skull!" John swerved, the cold sweat trickling down his back. He slammed on the brakes. "Keep going you fool. Keep going."

He punched the accelerator and the car leaped forward.

The engine protested and almost died on him but he managed to keep it going and hurtled past the luminous white skull by the side of the road.

"A cow. It's only a cow. A stupid big black cow with a white face."

Ruth giggled, with relief as much as anything. John's attempt at bravado was rather thin.

"I knew it was nothing," he said weakly.

"Oh yes? Well, why did you take that bend at sixty? You were going like a bat out of hell."

"I'm just anxious to find the place. I'm tired, I've been driving for hours."

But there was something in his voice which belied his words.

Night is a funny time. It's the time that your mind plays tricks on you. Or maybe not. Maybe daytime is the time in which the tricks are played. In the bright light of day we are brave, adults, grown-ups not afraid of shadows. But maybe that bravery is all a front – just maybe. If we were honest we would have to admit that we are afraid of the dark, of things that go bump in the night and the monster that lives, as we all know, under our beds. The real Ruth and John may have been the ones who, while driving through the night, felt like lost and frightened children, and who were frightened of a cow, and not, as they believed the confident, self-assured adults who programmed computers by day and played Trivial Pursuit by night.

So on they drove, each mile taking them farther from home, farther from the city where, to some extent, we can keep the dark at bay by means of streetlights and large stores with lit windows and glamorous mannequins reminding us that we are civilised, no longer cave people, no longer superstitious, reminding us of our modern day gods of commerce and sophistication.

Then out of the black a yellow beacon shone. A light, the first light, apart from their own headlights, for several miles. "Pull up here John and we'll take another look at the map. Can't be far now. Surely?"

Was there a hint of desperation in that word "Surely"?

They slowed down and were almost stopped when a figure,

a man, appeared out of nowhere. He came from the nearside and started pulling at the handle of the back door.

"Oh my God. He's trying to get into the car. John what are we going to do?"

John crashed the car into gear and sped off with a squeal of tyres and a crunching of gears. As they roared away Ruth looked out of the back window and saw a dapper little man in a military style blazer standing in the road looking after them. Who the hell was he? What did he want?

On and on they drove and there looked like no end in sight until eventually they came into a village. There was a pub and they decided that, driving or no driving, a stiff drink was what they both needed.

The pub was strangely unwelcoming. Oh, it had all the standard paraphernalia of a country pub and that should have made it nice enough. It had a log fire and a beamed ceiling, a fat jovial landlord and a throng of locals in the corner, but, or was it just them, there seemed to be something of an atmosphere. When they walked through the door it seemed as if they had interrupted something, a secret gathering maybe, or maybe just local malicious gossip.

They had a brandy each and a warm by the fire. They exchanged pleasant nods with the pub's original customers but there was something reluctant about it as if they sensed an intrusion. The stop at the pub did yield some information, they were only two miles away from West Mains Farm. They drained their glasses and left, their spirits somewhat raised by the spirits they had imbibed and by the information that their journey was drawing to a close.

Two miles has a habit of seeming a lot longer if you are desperate for your journey to end. After what seemed about ten miles they spotted a faint glow of light in the distance. This was West Mains Farm. Mrs Grant had sent them instructions as to how to get to the cottage, which was about one hundred yards down the track ... it would be misleading to call it a road.

They drew up outside a small cottage. The lights in the hall were on and the red flickering of a fire could be seen in what must have been the living room.

Was this the right place? There didn't seem to be any other

cottage in the vicinity but then if there were and if there were no lights on in it, they wouldn't see it anyway.

"Do you think this is it?"

"I suppose so."

"What shall be do?"

Ruth was brave.

"I'll knock the door and see what happens."

Nothing happened. She turned the handle and the door swung open.

"This must be the place. John, come on, let's go in."

As she looked round – John was unpacking the suitcase from the boot of the car – somewhere inside she felt unsure. It was like going into someone's house if you didn't know if they were in. She half expected to walk into the living room and be confronted by a stranger. People in the country left their doors unlocked. What if this was not their cottage. John was behind her now and he nudged her in with the suitcase.

"Are you sure it's all right?" she asked.

"This must be it. Come on. In we go."

In the hall there was a door to the right and the left. Ruth opened the door to the right the room was in darkness apart from the flickering of a fire. She turned on the light and they went exploring the house. The room on the left was the bedroom, a room off the living room, the kitchen, and upstairs another two bedrooms. There was no sign of anyone living there, no clothes in the wardrobe, no sheets on the upstairs beds, no food in the fridge. This must be the right place.

They were both tired, from the driving, and the fact that this was their first holiday in quite a few months. John brought a bottle of brandy from the suitcase and poured them each a large one.

Despite the brandy and the tiredness Ruth could not sleep. She kept waking from uncomfortable dreams with a sense of strangeness. John slept, as always, like a log, which made her uneasiness and feeling of being alone all the more acute. Around three o'clock, she got up and looked out of the bedroom window. There was very little to see. The night outside was black, like it can only be black in the middle of the night, in the middle of winter, in the middle of nowhere.

It was flat terrain outside, like bogland or moor. There was a low, moaning kind of sound coming from somewhere out in the darkness, it was impossible to say where, or even how far away it was. She shivered. She had never seen such black darkness before. At home, even with the curtains drawn shut and the lights off there was always the faint yellow glow of streetlights coming in through a chink somewhere. In this place only more darkness seeped in through the cracks. Suddenly there was a loud bang. Like a shot. She stood at the window listening. Nothing. She woke John up.

"Look, let's get out of here, I'm frightened. There is something really creepy."

John was tired. Too tired to drive but more than that, the outside, the darkness, the thought of driving round and lost in a circle frightened him more than staying put. Here at least they were warm, relatively secure. There was some sort of civilisation. After all, the farm wasn't that far away. Ruth returned to bed and they lay there huddled together for warmth. And moral support. They slept fitfully.

They were woken by a loud banging and the sound of footsteps outside in the hall.

"Oh, my God. What is it?" Ruth was panic stricken.

"Hello, hello," a voice from the hall called. "Are you there? It's me. Mrs Grant."

John opened the bedroom door and was confronted by Mrs Grant's smiling, ruddy features. Fat and jolly and the epitome of a farmer's wife. They looked out of the window. It was light. There was another cottage forty feet away from their own and the farmhouse just down the track. Suddenly they were amongst people when last night they had been so alone.

"I see you found us then? A lot of folk get lost."

Then they felt stupid. Childish. Like little lost children who have wandered to the next street and can't find their way home. "I hope you weren't disturbed by the bird scarer. It lets off a sound like a shot every now and again to keep them off the crops. I usually turn it off when there are people in the cottages but I forgot last night. Anyway it's off now."

They were sitting down to breakfast, sophisticated young people, pondering the events of the previous night. What about the man trying to get into the car? A drunk, maybe, who thought he recognised them, or maybe a bemuddled hitch-hiker. It seemed ridiculous in the cold light of day. The absurdly dapper old boy in the pitch black; their terror, his look of bewilderment. But it was over now. Normality had been reinstated. They wouldn't go back to that childish state of fear again. It was silly. They knew that now. They were people of the twentieth century, city dwellers, grown-ups.

Not afraid of the dark.

Maybe!

The Eternal Trapezoid

It was a long time ago, I know, but I think I can remember it. As near as I can remember it ...

Night. A campsite somewhere in East Europe, caravans in a semi circle, like in the westerns only these caravans are metal not canvas, not pulled by horses either. Yet horsepowered. Big lorries drag them and their inhabitants around various countries. So many it's difficult to know where you are at any given moment ... Night. Yes, I've said that but it's important. The lights in the caravans glow a sort of yellow light. The lights of a nearby town are whiter, sharper, like little needles of brightness. The stars do what they do everywhere, East Europe, America ... over the cowboys in their wagons and the Indians on their piebald ponies.

Three men sit in the fading red of a fire. It's mostly ashes and cinders now but there is enough light for them to see each other. They are having a conversation which goes something like this. Remember, I speak from memory.

Hans is the oldest of the three. He speaks first.

"I don't know how it happened. She just fell from my grip. I felt her hands slipping through mine. Oh my God, what have I done?"

If my memory serves me correctly he put his head in his hands at this moment. But then again, I may just have imagined this as it would seem to be the sort of thing he should do, or maybe that's what they do in the pictures. I'm not sure which. Lech is a handsome man about ten years younger than the first.

"Don't blame yourself, Hans. It was an accident. I too blame myself. If I had been there it might not have happened. What can we do now? How can we go on? Lola is dead. Beautiful Lola. How can we continue?"

Boris seems lost in his own thoughts and for a moment it appears he will not join this tortured conversation but at last he does.

"We must continue. What else can we do? We are nomads. We have nothing now except each other. Nothing to do but carry on."

The three men gaze into the fire. They say nothing for a long time. There is rustling as people in the background move stealthily about. Lights in the caravans go out one by one. The sky gets blacker as it gets later. Still they make no move as if to go. Then Hans gets up.

"Boris, Lech, excuse me I am going to bed."

The other two men sit on in silence. One is thin and frail-looking. His looks are misleading. Despite his wan face and skelf-like body, he is very strong and muscular. What is misleading is that he carries no excess weight. To call him wiry would be acceptable but not entirely accurate. A better comparison would be with that steel cable that holds up suspension bridges. Not enormously bulky, but incredibly strong. Lech, on the other hand, looks like an athlete. He is six feet tall, easy. If you were asked to guess his occupation and you only saw him fully dressed, you would say that he was a construction worker. If you knew something about construction you would say a scaffolder, maybe. You would say that because he has very well developed arm and shoulder muscles and scaffolders acquire such muscles from throwing scaffolding around all day. Unless he was wearing very tight trousers you would have failed to notice that his legs are very well developed too.

Lech is not a scaffolder, does not throw scaffold about. Does not throw anything about. Quite the reverse. Lech is a catcher.

Hans crosses in front of the fire and the two men and climbs the three steps to his caravan. His shadow can be seen by anyone who happens to pass, pacing up and down – anyone, that is, but Boris and Lech who have their backs to his caravan. The caravan he shared, until tonight, with Lola, his wife.

The catcher says to his companion, "Do you think he knows? Can he have guessed?"

"I don't know. He was acting strangely, even before the accident. After you left he was talking to himself."

"He was always nervous just before a performance."

"No, it was more than that. He was not himself. He rebuffed Lola twice. Even she noticed something was wrong. He said nothing. Just paced up and down as if something were on his mind."

"Oh God, how I regret the whole thing. I wish I had not walked out. So pointless. So petty. So selfish. I did not think of the act. I thought only of myself. I should have known you would not cancel the performance."

Boris looks sideways at Lech. Sympathy in his eyes. He shakes his head, almost imperceptibly.

"Lola insisted," he says.

This information does not help Lech.

"I know," he says, "I should have known Hans would be the catcher. Why didn't I think of that at the time? I just wanted to escape. To have time to myself to think."

"Where did you go?"

"To a bar – of all places. Somewhere in town, an empty cheerless place. I had imagined it would be different. I have seen bars from the outside. I thought them to be warm, hospitable places, full of good cheer and comradeship. This place was cold as the grave. I thought I would turn my back on you and Lola, that I would find companionship and warmth among strangers. I was wrong. I sat alone all night, only the bartender for company. Small groups huddled together but instead of spontaneous laughter and conversation, they bemoaned the cold and spoke of the onset of winter. They were as lonely and desperate as I was. I tried to hide from my life here. I thought I could turn my back on the circus, on the trapeze, on myself. Start again with someone new, someone who was not someone else's wife. Someone who was not Lola."

The smell, if you can imagine it, is the warmish smell of a late September night, the fecundity of greenery, lavender and thyme mingling with the wood smoke from the fire and the lingering cooking smell of onions, the hot rich smell of animals, horses, tigers, elephants. If asked I would say those smells existed but maybe Hans, Boris and Lech did not notice them. The smells they live with every day, after a while, they may no longer notice them any more than the farmer notices the reek of manure, the mechanic oil or the painter turpentine.

They are quiet for a few moments and then Boris speaks. "I feel guilty myself. After the fight I tried to find you, to ask you to come back. I know I hurt you with what I said. I meant it ... at the time. I'm sorry, was sorry even then. What you must understand is Lola was my twin, she was my life as much as I am myself. She was me also. That's how it is with twins. I could not stand to see her pulled apart. She was married to Hans, she could not be his wife and fulfil your love also. It was bad enough when she married him. I felt torn apart then, but to share her further, be hurt again, to share her three ways. No. It was too much to bear. I wanted it to be just her and me, like when we were small. Happily playing with the animals."

Yes, I can remember them too, two lonely, lovely children. Lola so sweet, playing with the dogs, learning to ride the horses. They were very close. Their parents died when they were very young and they were adopted by the troupe. No particular parents just whoever was around was their Mamma and Pappa. It sounds bad ... but no, they were happy. There was no shortage of love and I expect it made them closer. It was a wonderful life for children, they learned about the animals, helped out, or thought they did, cleaned the cages, the jugglers threw clubs to them, the bareback riders lifted them on to white ponies and they laughed as the horses jogged round and round. I can see them now, Lola her face upturned and laughing at Giuseppe the clown as he taught her the tricks of his trade. His own personal make-up, his trademark, each one is unique, you know. And she delighted in trying out the white and red grease paint sticks and laughing as she painted her small, round face. Boris standing by, watching, smiling, looking out for her, always looking out for his little sister who was all of ten minutes younger.

Even then a quiet boy, as if his parents' death had not only taken something very big from his young life but left something even bigger, left a responsibility for Lola, a demand, a need to grow up quick, to leave laughing behind and think not of himself but, first and foremost, of Lola. That sort of burden weighs very heavy on young shoulders and if Boris did not join in Lola's hearty, young, careless laughter, who would blame him?

Boris continues. "Why did you come back? I thought you never would. Especially now. What is there here for you now?"

"I had nowhere else to go. I thought when I left there might be an alternative. An outside world. Where could I go? A town like that?"

He nods towards the twinkling lights in the distance.

"I have no skills, no trade. I cannot mend shoes or wash windows. If someone asked me what I did for a living what would I say? I swing fifty feet in the air and catch, by the ankles, someone flying towards me. Useful, eh? I ply my trade – you do too – by risking my life, nightly, to amuse those who do useful things by day. I've never stayed in one town long enough to get to know the names of the streets. I've never slept in a house in my life. I could not sleep in a room that did not move with the wind. Those people, in the bar, are strangers to me. They care about things I have no use for: carpets, furniture, homes ... that means everything to them, their reason for working, living. I know nothing of that life. All I know and understand is here. I have no more choice than them. I risk my life every night and I don't know why. It's my job, that's all, my life. I have no money, no possessions and now not even Lola."

"Hans is taking it bad, Lech. He blames himself. He thinks he killed her. I tried to tell him, he won't listen. It was no-one's fault. We live our lives in the knowledge of death. One day. Any day, it might come. We all must share the guilt."

"No, Boris, I am the one. I left. I should have been here. I am the catcher. How could Hans be blamed? I should not have left. I am to blame. I am the catcher."

"But I chased you off, threatened you with violence, scandal, ridicule. I did it for selfish reasons, not because I wanted to defend Hans or to save their marriage, but because Lola loved you and that meant her love had to be divided even further. I was jealous. I hated you and I wanted to hurt you. In my pain, my striking out, I hurt the one person I loved most in the world. And all of us."

Boris rises and walks to the far end of the campsite and gazes up to the night sky. "Alive now. Tonight, but for me," he thinks and as he stands there dreaming he imagines he sees his sister. As he looks up he sees her, walking the tightrope, as she did as a young girl. She is carrying a parasol and as she reaches the middle, she falters, stumbles, almost falls, then regains her balance. Is Boris talking to her? Is he asking how she feels now, if at last she belongs, no longer an outsider? Safe in the knowledge that nothing more can harm her. Never again the terror that the next performance might be the last. No more tarnished sequins. Can she hear the animals? They sense death. They can smell it. They can't go back either. They are trapped just like their human trainers, both are caged. Set them loose in the jungle and they would not be able to fend for themselves. What would they do if their tamer did not bring them pounds of raw meat every day? They could not hunt. They don't know how. Just like the humans, where could they go? What could they do?

Lech had tried it, gone into town, to a bar, got drunk, but discovered that he had gone to a jungle. He was afraid and had come scurrying back to safety. This place, this campsite, inhabited by fire-eaters, midgets, giants and wild beasts is his home. This freak show which cannot stay in one place for more than a month is their haven, their security, all they have ever known. That's what people come to see. The lion closing its jaws round his tamer's head, the tightrope walker's fall. Next time the circus is in town it will be assured of a full house. They will be hoping to see another trapeze artist fall to the ground and for her blood to mingle with the sawdust, as on a butcher's floor.

Boris comes to the front of the campfire. Lech gets up and

joins him. Lech speaks first. "Were you talking to someone? I thought I heard voices?"

"No, just to myself. I was looking at the sky. It's funny – the stars always look the same to me. The sky is different, sometimes it's clear, sometimes misty, but the stars – always the same. We must have travelled thousands of miles, been in every country in Europe, but everywhere the stars look the same. I've always thought that I would like to study the stars. It would be nice to navigate by them, like sailors."

Lech put his arm round his shoulders.

"Boris my friend, let's stick to maps. We've enough problems without being lost as well."

They both laugh and the sound is strangely eerie in the quiet of the night.

As children they were happy. In fact they were happy until Hans joined the troupe. They would have been about thirteen. He came one winter. He arrived at night while they were asleep. No-one can remember where they were. In the morning he was just there and never went away again. Lola and Boris had been practising acts all their lives. They could do a bit of everything. Hans and Lola became very friendly. He started teaching her trapeze. They had done it before but not to performance standard. Boris pretended to be interested too because he did not want Hans to have her to himself. You see, she was all he had. Three years later Lola married Hans. Of course, a lot happened in between. They became an act.

I suppose some people might wonder if it was an accident at all. Could it have been deliberate? Could she have let go? Could Hans have let her fall? He had been behaving oddly before the performance. Did he know? Did he wonder why Lech had left so abruptly?

No-one who knew them could think that. Lola was incapable of guilt. She had the same effect on people as she had on animals – they would jump through hoops for her. She was beautiful, of course, and innocent and sweet and completely selfish. She looked on it as a right that she should be loved, that she could do what she wanted without fear of reproach. It must happen to many pretty girls, but because she was an orphan, even more so. Hans loved her like a father

23

loves a child, in a selfless way, he would have killed himself rather than stand in her way. How will he cope now? He blames himself. They all do.

In a dimly-lit caravan, Hans' shadow can still be seen pacing up and down. There is a knock at the door. Giuseppe the clown, enters.

"Can't sleep, eh, Hans?"

"No I've been trying to sort things out in my mind."

There is a candle burning in the window. It is for Lola's soul to find her way back. When they are gone from that place she will be able to follow the light. It's hard to believe that, just a few hours earlier, Lola had been laughing and prancing around the caravan in her glitter costume. The silly little sequined suit, small enough to be a child's, really. Now those little suits were hanging limply, pathetically, on a rail.

"Giuseppe, do you think tomorrow's performance will be cancelled?"

"I don't know. There was a crowd outside after ... you know. After tonight's show was stopped, demanding their money back. I think they were given tickets for tomorrow."

"My God, help me! My wife is dead and they want their money back ... There will be no time. That's what bothers me the most. No time to get adjusted. To do the petty things that need to be done. In a few days we will leave this place and not be back for years, maybe. Lola will stay here, among strangers. No Hans to visit her grave. No fresh flowers, she'll be alone. It's all so rushed. I would feel better if we had some rituals to observe – sending cards, that sort of thing. Those petty rituals would keep my hands busy and my mind from dwelling."

Later on, late into the night, Hans had other visitors, a giant who had to stoop and could not stand upright in the caravan, a midget whose feet swung about aimlessly as he sat in the chair. Outsiders, strange, roaming people who had come to try to share, and therefore reduce the grief. No-one could help Hans much but it was good of them to try and he appreciated it. He was alone and it would not have mattered where he was or what he did for a living, it was nothing to do with being with the circus. He would have been just as alone anywhere. Boris and Lech were alone too. We are all alone in this world.

Two days later, the campsite was empty. The circus had moved on. It went like a glowworm in the night, a little train of lights, a constellation of stars roaming round the heavens for all eternity.

Night Out

It was a women's night out. And all that that entails. Too
much drink. Too little sense. Not that a men's night out
would be any better. Worse, more than likely. Anyway, I
rolled home about midnight, good times were had by all. Let
the good times roll. Into the flat, up the stairs, none too
cleverly, concentrating madly on each stair. Christ, it's a hard
life. Well, climbing stairs is hard when you're three sheets to
the wind. Three sheets? One over the eight sheets and then
some! Quietly into the flat. Take shoes off at the outside
door. Creaking boards. Shit. It's all very well having bare
floor boards sanded and varnished, but trying to creep in
without waking the better half! It ain't easy. Into bed.
Carefully now, pull down the duvet. Don't make a sound.
Ah, great, he's still asleep. Don't want to wake him. Not fair.
Pull the covers up over your head. Room spinning? I know,
but it will pass. Quiet. Shit! This is when I always remember
I should have drunk four pints of water to avert a hangover
in the morning. No, I'll be fine. Haven't drunk that much.

Almost asleep but there is some noise; can't quite place it.
Next door? No. Outside? Never mind, forget it, go to sleep.
Head a bit fuzzy. Concentrate on sleeping. Sleep will come.
Always does.

"Hmm, urg."

Oh, now he's moving. Don't wake him. Not fair. Work
early in morning. Lie like a corpse. Fine, he's gone back to
sleep. What is that fucking noise? It just won't go away. Shut
your ears. Concentrate, go to sleep. HMMM ... mind going
blank, then silly ideas. Illogical things happening inside my

27

head. Good, that means I'm falling asleep. What in the name of God is going on out there? Voices. But not from a house. Voices outside. What are voices doing outside at midnight? Laughing! Shit, some people have no consideration. Go to sleep.

"No, mummy. No. Mummy, no. I don't like it mummy. No!"

What is going on out there? I must get up. Open the window. Lean out. A child crying.

"No. I don't like it. No!"

Fuck sake! What the Hell. Go out. It's coming from the other side of the lane. Wake him up? No. Probably nothing. Phone the police? Say, "Look, I'm sorry to bother you but ... I think ..." No. What could I say? Nothing tangible. Go outside, see what's happening. Down the stairs. Out the door to the back. Pitch black. Beginnings of fear. Dutch courage wearing off. Up and down the lane. Still the voices. Still the child crying but can't work out where it's coming from but it's definitely coming from one of the gardens on the other side of the lane. Out the lane and down the street, desperately trying to work out how the backs of these flats correspond to the back of mine. Halfway up the hill. No, too far. Must be down about number 42. In through the close. Door to the back green locked. Listen at the door. Nothing. Back to the lane walking up and down. Nothing. Voices seem to have died down. Back up the stairs into the flat, more creaking boards, more tiptoeing. Back to the bedroom. Look out the open window again. Flickering. Red flickering. A fire. Child crying. Now just sobbing. Brain beginning to clear a bit. All that fresh air and fear diluting the vodka. This is bloody stupid. Still, there is no way I can sleep now. Phone the police. Say what? There is a child crying somewhere, don't know where, or why. Fat lot of good. Think I'm a loonie. Busy people. Waste of time.

Oh shit, nothing else for it. Out again into the lane. This time I have a fair idea of where the fire is. Madskulls having a barbeque at fuckin' one o'clock in the morning. Pitch black spiral stairs again down to the back. Probably fall down these bloody stairs and break my bloody neck. Just like the thing. Imagine the papers. What would my mother think?

"DRUNK WOMAN FALLS DOWN STAIRS AND BREAKS STUPID NECK. Can't imagine what she was doing out there at that time of night, says heart-broken spouse."

All right for him ... at least it's just his heart that's broken. It's my bloody neck. Anyway, I've safely negotiated the stairs. Neck intact. Out into the lane. There is a section with some garages. Down I go. I can see the flames flickering. Women talking. I creep up to the wall. It's a witches' coven. Obviously. What else could it be? Women, fires, sacrificing children in some terrible ritual. If I strain I can hear what they are saying.

"So I says tae him. Well that's all there bloody is. If you don't like stew, well that's your tough luck."

"Tough luck and tough stew, eh?"

Laughter.

"Right you. Watch it. There's nuthin' wrang wi' ma cooking."

"Nuthin' that a flamethrower wouldnae fix."

More laughter.

The windows in the flat above are lit. This is a strange conversation for a witches' coven. An odd place to hold it, too. Surely the people in the flats with the lit windows can see everything that goes on. And the child has stopped crying. What to do now? Stand around for a few minutes; see if anything happens. More conversation. Dull, banal stuff. No more children crying. Back upstairs. Into bed. Sleep. Eventually.

Next morning and for a few mornings scour paper for news of witches' coven in the southern suburbs of the city. No news. No children crying in the night either. Everything must be OK.

I suppose.

Hooch Was His Password

Richard Slicker, the slick dick, private investigator and public bar habitué, free-lance journalist, free thinker, freeloader and three-time loser, strolled into the office. A murmur rippled round the newsdesk. He was that kinda guy. The kind that got served first in the only oasis in the Sahara. The type of guy who walked into a crowded bar, and with the raise of an eyebrow, had the waiter pushing his way through the throng to deliver a double bourbon on a silver tray complete with a single red rose in a crystal vase, while the hoi polloi waved their arms and stomped their feet and gnashed their teeth in an effort to catch the barman's eye. Dick was eyecatching.

He strolled across the newsroom of the Daily Enquirer. A slow languid gait, slightly splay-footed and lazily scuffing his feet on the wooden floor. He was saved from being slovenly, only by the uprightness of his carriage. His lightweight jacket, slung casually over his shoulder, was kept there by a crooked index finger acting as a surrogate hook. He slumped into his chair. On his desk, in front of him, a visual display unit. He typed his secret password into the system to get himself and the computer on the same wavelength. His password was 'Hooch'. It was as secret as The Pope's religion.

To his immediate right was his colleague and long-time boozing buddy Vincent O'Rare. Vince had been, at various times, novice priest and semi-pro boxer. The fighting plus a lifetime of drinking had left its mark on his face. He had studied for the priesthood for a year until he discovered that his vocation leant more towards drinking than God. In the meantime he had fallen head-over-heels in love with a dame, so that was the celibacy out the window too. The femme used to call him "The fighting Tim O'Rare" but when he left the Catholic church to become a Buddhist she gave him the heave. If there was one thing she could not stand it was a Turner.

"Anything doing, Vince?" Dick asked. Vince looked almost harassed.

"Chrissake Dick, where have you been for the last twenty four hours, practising to be an ostrich? That broad, Marileen MacDonald, the one that's shooting that film downtown, she's disappeared. Just walked off the set and hasn't been seen since. Every newshound in the city is on the lookout for her. That dame is big news even if she's just taking a leak.

"Sonny Scarface Francisco has jumped bail. The airports and train stations are crawling with lawmen but the clever money is on him hiding out somewhere in the city. He has a dame here, no one knows who she is but the word on the street is he's crazy about her and that's why he jumped. Oh yeah, and someone phoned looking for you. Dolores, I think she said her name was."

Dick's heart jumped inside his ribcage. Now that WAS news. His hand jerked toward the phone to return her call but he stopped it halfway and put it back in his pocket. He pulled out a cigarette case and assumed a nonchalant air. There are two things that Dick Slicker never runs after. Dames and buses. If you miss one there will always be another along in a minute.

He took a drag on his fag, seconds dragged by. He was desperate to phone. He was desperately affecting an unconcerned attitude. It was too much for him; he winked at Vince.

"Must mollify the moll," he rasped. Vince grunted an agreement.

The phone rang eight times before Dolores answered. It seemed like an eternity. Eventually he heard a click and a voice like molasses said, "Hello. This is Miss Dolores Devine speaking."

"Hi Dol. This is Dick. Howya, honey?"

She sounded out of breath, as if she had been running.

"I was in the shower, I'm dripping all over the floor. I've got nothing on but a towel."

Molasses yea! the second it turns into rum. Hot and rough and packs a kick like a mule. His breathing was like a schoolboy. It came in short pants. This dame was hot as the devil's hearth and twice as dangerous.

"What ya doin'? I'm finished here round about tennish. Want to meet me in town? Great. See ya."

He hung up the phone. He had some work to do and he would have to motor to get through it in time. He set to work to write up his copy, a mundane sort of thing about a guy who wrapped himself, and his Porsche, round a lamppost. A large man appeared at his side.

"Oh, no, it's the death-watch beetle," Dick whispered to Vince, "and it looks as if it's me he will be tapping. I still haven't got back the tenner I lent him last month."

But for once the death-watch beetle wasn't tapping.

"Type! Type!"

He was shouting. Dick tried to ignore him, the only type he was interested in was the red-headed ones with too much in the way of legs and too little in the way of brains, but the news editor would not be put off.

"Type up that goddamned story before it misses the goddamned edition."

Editions, editions, this guy's vocabulary was strictly limited, but Dick did as he was bid.

The rest of the shift was quiet and no more news came in about the starlet or the gangster so about 9pm Dick decided to leave.

"If any dame should phone," he told Vince, "say I'm in the caseroom and you can't get hold of me. I'm going down to Big Eddie's for a swiftie."

He swung out of the office and into the big wrought iron lift. "Going down?" the lift attendant asked.

"Ain't I always, Pop? Or at least that's what my young lady tells me."

On the editorial floor Dick's phone was ringing. Vince picked it up. No, Dick was not in the office. No, he didn't know when he would be back. No message? OK. Goodbye. The phone clicked. Vince hung up. Marileen MacDonald replaced the receiver at her end and looked at the bedside table. It had the ubiquitous Gideon Bible, the equally ubiquitous bottle of sleeping pills and a letter and phone number. The letter said if you are in trouble get in touch with my buddy on the Enquirer and the phone number was Dick's.

He shouldered his way to the bar.

"Hi, Eddie. Give me a large one and don't go away. I've a feeling I'll be needing a refill pretty soon."

He downed the drink in one and then had the refill. This one he sipped and made it last five minutes.

"One for the road, Ed. I'm meeting the doll and I don't want to turn up the worse for wear. On the other hand I don't want to turn up sober either, so make it a double."

He went out into the night street. The place was a hubbub. Piles of newspapers were being bundled into vans. Large, loud, sweaty individuals were shouting, throwing each other parcels of newspapers and snippets of patter. There was a small but constant stream of people coming and going through the front door of the newspaper building. Reporters with big stories, printers dropping into Big Ed's for a break, cleaners and chefs coming off and going on duty. This place was just coming to life when everyone else was thinking of turning in.

The building was a large, black glass pile, five floors high but only one lift. The lighted editorial floor ran round the centre of the building like a silver coachline on a black limousine. On his desk inside his phone was ringing. Dick chucked his half-smoked cigarette into an oily puddle beside a delivery van and sloped off in the direction of "The Roof Garden" where he hoped Dolores would be waiting.

Dolores was perched on the edge of a high bar stool. She looked as if she might topple at any minute, but of course she wouldn't. Her tottering, almost out of control act, was just that, an act. Dolores had more control than the President of the United States and was better looking, too. She was wearing a red sheath dress, backless and very nearly frontless and split to the thigh. There was so little of her in it that there was almost no point in wearing it. Except, of course, that was exactly the point in wearing it. She never carried a purse.

Why the Hell should she – all the collateral she would ever need was stacked inside the red sheath dress. She looked a million dollars. And I don't mean green and wrinkled. She was laughing and when she laughed she parted a red, almost perfect, mouth to reveal white, absolutely perfect white teeth. A martini glass on the bar in front of her had on the rim an almost perfect red imprint of her almost perfect mouth.

She was laughing with, and talking to, some greasy looking guy with a scar on his face. Dick didn't like that one bit, but even more he didn't like anyone to know he didn't like it. He sauntered up to her and put his arm round her waist and kissed the back of her head. The hair on the back of his neck stood on end, or was it hackles? He looked at the greaseball and smiled. He enquired if anyone wanted a drink. He ordered a fresh martini for Dolores and a large bourbon for himself.

The greaseball was now engaged in conversation with a rough looking guy on his left. Dolores looked into Dick's eyes. They were glazed and having difficulty focusing but they still had a devilish glint.

"Honey. Don't you think you've had enough to drink?" she said. "Why don't I take you home and you can get some shuteye?"

"I ain't had that much, Baby, maybe five?"

He omitted to mention that the five had been doubles and the hip flask he kept in his desk was empty. There was a pint of whisky inside him and nothing else.

"I don't have a drinking problem. 'Cept when the bars are closed."

He looked at Dolores and she was whispering something to the greaseball. He thought he caught the last word. He thought it was Honey. He pulled himself up to his full six two and said, "Hey greaseball! You tryin' to muscle in on my dame?"

The rough meat on the other side made a move but a diamond clad hand on his shoulder restrained him.

"It's OK, Frankie. Leave this to me."

The greaseball stood up. He was not a tall man. No more than five nine, but wiry. He was expensively dressed and toting a couple of grand worth of sparklers on his hands.

When he spoke it was like someone was grinding coffee beans.

"Listen buddy," he said. "I ain't lookin' for no trouble, however, I never turn my back on it. What say you we forget the whole thing?"

Dick had five inches over the guy, but there was something in the cold, hard, stare, the dead fish eyes that told him to back off. He did it with as much dignity as he could muster and allowed Dolores to take him home.

When they got back to his flat she undressed him and put him to bed. While he slept he dreamt he was fighting with the rough meat and in the course of the fracas got hit over the head with a bottle. He woke at six-thirty. Dolores was in the kitchen, making coffee.

"I feel awful, Baby," he said. "As if I've been hit on the head with a bottle."

"You have," she said. "But not on the outside."

She left for work before he could find out any more about the events of the previous night. He searched the flat for some booze, he figured that there should be about half a bottle stashed away somewhere. There always was, just in case. He found the stash and took a long hard slug out of the bottle. The bottle slugged him back. He was feeling better already. Now he was in good shape again and ready to go trouble shooting. If he could turn up some news on the starlet or bailjumper, that type of information would be bound to be worth plenty. The best place to uncover information like that was in a bar, not any old bar, but certain bars, where certain people hung out. The type who keep their eyes and ears open and are prepared to sell anything for the price of a drink. Dick knew these bars well.

He slipped out, bought himself a breakfast, a shave and another half bottle ... just in case. He would finish the first half bottle then have a sleep until opening time, then go to work.

He slept 'til noon, then had a wash and put on a clean white shirt, navy blue, double breasted suit and maroon tie with parrots. He might as well dress down, there was no need to look conspicuous. He went into the "Green Parakeet" for a drink. He looked about as inconspicuous as a giant in a top hat at a dwarfs' convention. He ordered a large one and went to the phone.

"Hi, Vince. Dick here. Any news?"

"Well the starlet turned up. Dead. In a hotel room. A bottle of barbiturates inside her and the phone in her hand. Some dame was calling you all night. I gave her the usual line. She sounded kinda desperate, I was half-tempted to tell her where to get hold of you but you know what you told me about dames, once you let them got hold of the idea they can contact you whenever they like, you may as well be dead. They're never off your back."

"Thanks, Vince. You did great. See you later."

There was no murmur on the street. He hung around various dives all day but nothing. It seemed Sonny Francisco had everyone trussed up like Christmas turkeys and everybody knows them birds don't sing. Around about the cocktail hour he found himself in a long, narrow bar. Outside there was a red neon sign and the doorway was black; in his fuzzy, hazy, drink addled mind, it reminded him of Dolores. He went to the payphone and called her.

"Hi, Dol. I'm in Nathan's. How soon can you get here?" He went back to the bar and ordered a long drink. Dick could drink with anyone, he prided himself on that fact, but today he had packed quite a lot in and Dolores don't like drunks, he better slow up a bit. Half an hour later she arrived. She didn't look too pleased to see him propped up on the bar.

He tried to explain that he had been working and that hanging around in bars was part of the job and if he didn't drink he would blow his cover. Anyway, he thought that's what he was saying but between it going from his mouth to his brain and back to his ears, it might have lost something. It sounded like a slurred babble. He tried again, only this time he might have missed out something really important so he said it again.

Dolores turned on her heel and went straight for the phone box. A minute later she was back. She was trying to tell him something very, very earnestly. He didn't pick it up. She was saying something about Sonny Francisco but he wasn't sure what. He had this idea that she had heard something on the grapevine and she was trying to tell him. Hell. She was a swell gal. She had dug up the info he needed. He could kiss her. He tried. She side-stepped and he fell off the stool. While he was picking himself up he noticed she had a small suitcase at her feet. He levered himself up on it. He must phone over the copy. No matter how drunk he was, he never lost his newspaperman's instincts. He lurched over to the phone. He phoned the newsdesk. Vince wasn't there. He told the guy on the phone that he had a big story and that he would be in shortly to file it. Strangely, he didn't seem all that interested. Dick had not even finished the message, when he heard the phone click and the line go dead. The young punk had hung up on him. Dick Slicker. He would show them, they would be sorry once the story was filed. He, with the help of Dolores, had managed to get the story everyone was chasing.

As he lurched out of the booth he saw the small greaseball punk come through the door, walk up to Dolores, put his arm round her waist and pick up the suitcase. She called him something. What was it? Sounded something like Honey. A slurred version, sort of like Shunny, odd, she didn't usually slur. Maybe she had been drinking too. Only she didn't usually drink much. What was happening? Dolores and the greaseball walked to the door. Just before they left she turned round. "Goodbye Dick," she called.

Well, there goes my story, he thought. I've nothing to file now. I'll just leave a message and then go home and get some sleep. I expect Dolores will be back later.

He phoned the newsroom. Everyone, he was told by the switchboard, was too busy to take his call. He left a message with them.

"Nothing to report. Will phone when anything turns up. Don't worry, nothing gets past Dick Slicker."

One Saw Stars

"I'm sorry that staircase is not for the public's use ... Oh I'm sorry Mrs Gray, I didn't know it was you. Meeting Mr Gray?"

"Hello Davie. No I'm here on business today. A witness for the prosecution. Is it OK if I use the stairs? I'm terrified of lifts. A big wean, really."

"Och aye. Away up ye go. It's the witness muster area yer after. Know where it is, do you?"

"I'll find it OK, Davie, don't worry."

It has its advantages knowing the security guards. I really am frightened of lifts and in this court they don't allow the public to use the stairs in case the accused meets the Sheriff and banjos him. Having a husband who is an advocate helps in the battle against lift-using.

I manage to find the witness muster area, which is quite surprising because I have absolutely no sense of direction at all. It's fairly sparsely populated and I look round for a quiet spot. I do this automatically now. I find it hard to be rude to people. I hate talking to strangers but I appear to act as a magnet for the most garrulous people in the world. So it simplifies my life if I sit in a corner out of the way of everyone. I always carry a book, which I have my nose buried in, but sometimes not even that works. Usually, there is one persistent character who simply will not leave me alone and insists on extracting my life story or bores me to death with his.

"Hot in here, eh, hen?"

"Yes, so it is."

I returned to my book but it was no good.

"It's probably because we are all so nervous."

"Yes."

Me nervous. Fat chance. Even if I had the propensity to be nervous, which I don't ... all these years of Gerry practising his interrogation techniques on me ... all those times, before we were married, in the public gallery watching him in action would have knocked it out of me. Not to mention the dress rehearsal we had last night, with Gerry doing his Perry Mason bit and conjuring up identical twin brothers from Australia to flummox me. No, when I get into that witness box, the Great Defender-himself, Marshall Hall, could not unnerve me.

However ... I went into the court and looked around. I saw him sitting in the dock between two policemen. He looked so small and white. He was absolutely ashen. I had rehearsed, in my head, how I would deflect the defence's questions.

"Mrs Gray," he would say, "how long ago did the offence take place?"

"Almost two years ago."

"And for how long, would you say, did you get the chance to have a proper look at the defendant?"

"About a minute."

"And are you still certain, Mrs Gray, after two years, that this is the man you saw, for a minute, that day?"

"Yes."

"How can you be so sure?"

At this point, in my head, I would look directly at him in the dock. Look him straight in the eye and say, "I remember him so clearly because he is a strikingly handsome man!"

Defence in ruins. Anyway, what really happened was that when the prosecution asked me to point him out, I looked over at him, staring straight in front, his face blanched and my heart went out to him. I raised my arm to point to him and it started to shake uncontrollably. I only just managed to get the words out. My voice almost deserted me. At this point the Sheriff decided to have a break for coffee and I was shown into a room on my own.

I sat there shaking. It's all very well in theory identifying someone but when you have to stand up and look them in the eye, point to them and say, "It was him", it fair takes the breath away from you. Suddenly, the defendant becomes a human being. You can see him swallowing and you know exactly how you would feel in his place.

I thought about what the defence might say. I dithered with the idea of sounding so unsure that the jury would have qualms. In the end I wrestled with my conscience and decided that the only thing to do was to tell the truth. It was him. I knew it was him. I recognised him. He was a strikingly handsome man.

I went back in after the coffee break. I looked over at him. He looked right back and yes, he was indeed a handsome man. Not overly tall but very dark, beautiful brown eyes, collar length black hair, the odd stray grey one, a bit of the Romany in him maybe.

In the end the defence had no questions for me. I think he had given up on his client. After I had given my evidence he changed his plea to guilty and everybody got to go home. I was a hero.

I couldn't get him out of my thoughts. Gerry and I went to a Mozart concert that night and during the interval I looked out of the window. It was Midsummer Eve. The longest day. *He* would spend the shortest night of the year in jail. I wondered if it would feel short to him.

Later, over the Chinese meal, I explained everything to Gerry. He understood, of course, he was used to it but I had done the right thing. The only thing. Why should I feel guilty? *He* was the criminal.

Next morning I decided to visit him in prison. I was a volunteer prison visitor, an advocate's wife and a friend of the governor. I would have no problems getting in or being allowed to see him in private for a couple of minutes. I would explain to him why I had to do it, tell him to make use of his time to good effect, inform him of all the reforming pursuits he could get up to.

I had worked it all out in my head. Again, it bore as much resemblance to what really happened as my inter-cranial court appearance had.

I would visit him. He would be hostile at first, of course, but after a while he would come round. I would show him the error of his ways. He would take an Open University degree, write a best-selling novel and dedicate it to me as his saviour. "To Mrs Gillian Gray," it would read, "without whose help I would still be a petty criminal." That sort of thing!

He refused to see me. How was I going to rehabiliate him now? I sat outside for hours while negotiations went on. I had almost given up when he eventually agreed. I had clout. I knew the governor. Whether he put pressure on him or whether it was the bribe of two hundred fags, I don't know. If it was the bribe it was hardly the best footing for a rehabilitation. Anyway, I got to see him. In a small cell-like room. There was a table in the middle of the floor and a chair on either side.

I asked the warder to stay outside. He was reluctant but eventually got the OK from my pal the governor. I would call out if I needed him.

"Hello Alec. Can I call you Alec?"

"Fuck off."

"Look I'm sorry ..."

"Fuck off."

He was standing with his back to me. One hand leaning on the corner of the table. He didn't even turn round to abuse me. He just stood with his back to me, urging to leave.

"I wanted to see you."

"Aye. Right, fine. You've seen me. Now fuck off."

"Please. Look. I'm sorry. What could I do?"

"Right, fine. Ye did the right thing. Fuck off."

He turned round to face me. I just looked at him. I couldn't stop. There was something about him. His whole body was stiff, the muscles taut and straining, his brown eyes cold and dead. He hated me. I did not blame him. He exuded pent-up anger and frustration. His teeth were clenched, his fists were clenched. He was standing flat-foot on the ground, legs apart, as if balancing himself in case I suddenly leapt at him. No danger of that happening, of course, and well he knew it, but that defensive/aggressive stance was obviously second nature to him.

I found myself uncontrollably glancing down to the front of his trousers. No stiffness there but a respectably sized bulge all the same. I looked back at his cold, hard, brown eyes. There were slight wrinkles at the side of his eyes, laughterlines, but he certainly wasn't laughing at the minute.

"What the fuck do you want?"

I couldn't help it, my eyes automatically went down to his crotch again. I forced them up to meet his cold, hard stare. He moved towards me and I heard myself gasp out loud.

"It's aw right. Don't worry. I'm no' going to attack you. I'm no' that daft. I know who you are. Pal of the governor. Husband some big wig. Yer safe with me."

I wondered if he punned deliberately. He moved closer and I caught a whiff of him. He had the smell that men acquire when they have washed recently but not too recently. The smell they have when they don't cover it with aftershave. The mannish smell of him caught me unawares. I was aware that I was standing staring at him with my mouth slightly open and I was breathing slightly too hard through it.

"Yer safe with me." Was that what he had said? That phrase, which should denote security, had a menacing ring. And not just for obvious reasons. Not because he was frightening me with unspoken, denied violence, but because he was threatening me with unspoken and undenied sexuality. He walked over to me, slowly, and I held my breath. I backed away, he still came. Eventually, I had my back to the wall and nowhere to go. I looked at the door and noticed that I had backed into a part of the room that could not be seen through the peep hole in the door. I must have looked terrified because he reassured me again that he would not harm me. He leant one arm against the wall, I could feel his breath on my face, I could smell the warmth of his body. I felt my chest heaving. He looked down and saw it too.

"Yer frightened."

"No."

"Why all the heavy breathing – I won't touch you." He paused for a long time and then said, "Promise."

I put my arm up to try to push him away and when I felt his hard, muscular body under the rough prison shirt my knees almost folded up under me. I pushed him as hard as I could but it made no impression on him. He just kept staring at me with those deep, hard eyes. This close I could see the long black eyelashes and the suggestion of stubble on his chin. I still had my hand on his stomach, trying to get him away, still not succeeding. I put my other hand on his left side and did a bit of pointless struggling. His body felt good under his clothes, lean, muscular, hard. I could see a few wisps of black, curly hair at the point where his shirt was open. His sleeves were rolled up and strong arms with dark skin and silky black hair were leaning on the wall just at the height of my shoulders.

He looked down at my chest heaving up and down again. At this point, I should have removed my hands altogether but I didn't. I stopped pushing and just left them on his body, feeling his gentle breathing.

I looked into his eyes and licked my lips. He licked his lips too and as I saw his tongue flick out a charge of electricity surged through my whole body. I was having difficulty standing up. My legs, jelly-like, were not up to the challenge. I was leaning on him, my arms on his shoulders, my legs crumpling up under me.

I looked down again at his crotch. He was not as unaffected as he appeared. My hand slowly went from his shoulder to his chest, over the hard stomach that pushing all my weight against hadn't moved, and down farther, down to the waistband of his regulation trousers, down to the bulge. I paused just before I got to it. He looked me right in the eye and did not flinch.

There was a noise outside the door and I panicked. I tried to shove him away, again to no avail.

"Someone will come in," I said.

"You told them not to disturb you. They're your pals."

"No, please. Stop."

He took a long finger and put it to my lips, moving it round the outline, very slowly.

"Sshh," he said quietly. And my knees turned to jelly again.

He leant down, not too far because he was only a couple of inches taller than me, but he bent down and pressed his lips against mine, gently. So gently I could hardly feel them. Then suddenly, quickly his tongue darted out and pressed its way into my open mouth. I put one arm round his waist and the other round his shoulder and pulled him towards me.

Panting and gasping we were grinding lips, not kissing, and every once in a while our teeth clashed. Desperately, he was reaching up my skirt and I took my right arm away from his middle and tried to push it away.

"No. No. You can't. Please. Stop. Please!"

"Sshh."

I felt a cold finger in a warm place. I felt as if there was electricity running through the finger into me and surging through my entire body. He had found it. In one go. Immediately, no fumbling, no searching, no false starts. Christ, my bloody husband had difficulty in finding my clitoris and this ... stranger had honed in on it at once. I closed my eyes and just let wave after wave of pleasure surge through me. He was stroking and flicking and massaging in turns. He could do it better than I could myself. Then I felt something hot. I looked down and his trousers were at his knees and his hot, pulsating cock was pressing against me. I couldn't see it, his shirt was covering it, but I felt the immense heat and smelled the sweet, hot mugginess of it. He had positioned it so that the head was poised at the mouth of my vagina.

"No. No. You can't. Please." But even as I was saying it my shaking legs and panting breath was giving me away. I wanted it bad and he knew it. I had my arms round his neck and he was holding my waist. I moved my right leg slightly further right, my left leg slightly further left and bent my knees fractionally. He understood. He slipped his hands round and placed them one on each buttock. A quick thrust and he was inside me. My God, what a feeling! Don't let anyone ever tell you that size does not matter. It matters. He was perfect. He was big enough to completely fill me, stretching me ever so slightly, but not too big to hurt me. He felt wonderful. I told him.

"Oh, fuck."

"I will, don't worry baby."

He was moving slow and hard. Even so, I knew he couldn't last long. I felt my orgasm starting. It came from my toes and I knew it would take another ten seconds for it to get where it was going. I just had to pray he would last that long. At that moment, he gave out a low, moan-like grunt that sounded as if it came from the bowels of the earth, from a prehistoric animal, a primeval sound that men have been making since the dawn of time. I knew that moan could not be held in any more than the white breaker of come which would inevitably follow it. My orgasm came. I came, my vagina went into a spasm. It contracted and held him while he threw his head back and issued a huge silent howl that filled the room. Shuddering and juddering, we collapsed on each other. Him still holding me up, me now supporting his head on my shoulder.

He looked up and I looked into his eyes. They had misted over with pleasure. There was silence for a few moments.

"Can I call you Alec now?" I asked him. He smiled slightly, almost imperceptibly. His eyes crinkled at the corners and he showed some white teeth.

"You look nice when you smile. You should try it more often."

"I've not had much to smile about recently."

He consented to me coming back the next week. He was not particularly enthusiastic about it.

"If ye want," was all he said.

On the way home I felt strange. Strangely satisfied, happy, in a mindless, post-sex way, but at the back of my mind was the absurdity of it. It was stupid and reckless. This man was the criminal and I was an advocate's wife. It was madness but I was driven on by something bigger than respectability, or convention. I was driven on by pure lust. My clitoris was ruling my head and I loved it. I luxuriated in remembering the feeling inside when he came. I remember the way his longish wavy, black hair, swept back from his face and stayed in place when he threw his head back in a moment of ecstasy. I remembered with delight playing with it when he rested his head on my shoulder. I almost couldn't drive I was tingling so much.

A sordid routine set in. Every Friday I would go, sexy underwear under my conservative suit, to the jail. I would take a book because he had taken an English course. It was mainly a front but we were both enjoying it. I would take little presents to keep the warders sweet – cigarettes, the odd bottle of whisky. Yes, bribery and corruption were added to my list of sins.

One Friday, he was performing his usual weekly miracle with his tongue and lips. I was standing in "Our Corner", he was kneeling in front of me. Suddenly, I looked down and felt a wave of pity for him.

"Alec."

He looked up but kept on doing what he was doing. I put my hands on either side of his face and plucked him off, like a baby off the breast.

"I'm sorry," I said.

"Hmmm." He tried to return to his task but I didn't let him.

"No, listen. Really. I'm sorry."

"I forgive you."

"No. LISTEN. I mean for ... you know, in court ... that time. I'm sorry, Alec."

He just looked up at me from his knees. "It was worth it." He went back to his cunnilingus.

I thought about that when I got home. "It was worth it." He was a man of very few words. Certainly not much in the way of lovey dovey, soppy stuff or endearments but that small phrase took the wind from my sails. I thought about him, on his knees, in prison. Me holding his face and him looking up like a child.

I sat for a long time thinking about him. I was roused from my dream by the phone ringing.

"Hello."

"Hello. Mrs Gray, would you like to comment on the allegation that you are having sex sessions with a prisoner in Barlinnie?"

Oh my god. Panic. How could the papers have found out? A warder, one of those bloody screws ... take the bribe but talk to the press anyway. How did they know? Was it that obvious what we were doing? I suppose it must have been. Oh shit. What the fuck will I do now?

"Mrs Gray ... Mrs Gray ..."

The Best Man

It was before the days of underwater weddings where the bride and groom wear scuba diving suits; before the nuptials could be blessed fifty feet up in a hot air balloon; even before garden marquees, country hotels, or even, for us, the co-operative halls. The bride was the baby of the family, the youngest of seven, her father long since dead, her mother housebound. The groom was an orphan, his only living relatives somewhere in Ireland. In those days weddings, for us, consisted of a nice dress and a church. No sumptuous meal, no toasts, no disco, no going away outfit, favours or chucked bouquets. No Rolls Royce. A taxi took the bride and her groom to her mother's home, a squalid two room and kitchen with a black sink and brass swan's neck tap in the kitchen. Ancient curtains sagging on string only just met as they stretched across the window. Faded linoleum on the floor.

The guests followed on the bus. On a makeshift table in the corner a buffet was laid out. Ham sandwiches, sausage rolls, Blue Riband biscuits, a couple of Lyons frosty layer cakes (one strawberry, one lemon) cut into thin slices. The men drank beer, the women tea and towards night everyone would have a singsong. I don't even think there was a gramophone.

The best man proved to be highly popular, tall and handsome with shining eyes and a Tony Curtis hairdo. He was a great jiver. Everyone said. He danced with all the women, flattering them as he did so, smiling his smile. Joked with the men. The life and soul of the party. He constantly asked the bride's mother to sing.

"Come on, Rose," he would say, "let's hear one of your old Irish tunes." She would oblige, smiling like a girl, and sing Come Back Paddy Reilly To Bally James Duff, The Mountains of Mourne or I Met Her in the Garden Where the Praties Grow. Later on she amazed him with her lilting and he amazed everyone by saying he had never heard the mouth music before. We could not believe that everyone was not put to sleep by it in their cradle or heard it in the background as potatoes were being peeled.

Everyone took turns to sing: Christie did his Elvis impersonation, Sean sang *Ole Man River* even lower than Paul Robeson, Patsy did her party piece: placed a banana on her head, wrapped a tablecloth round her waist, swung her hips and sang *We're Having A Heatwave*. Mary, my mother, sang *It's Only a Paper Moon*. We were all sitting in a circle in the tiny living room and round the circle we went, taking turns at singing.

We were a family of singers; it was well known. Ronnie, the best man, was eventually persuaded to sing. He sang *I Believe* in an unbelievably beautiful, clear, bell-like voice. There wasn't a dry eye in the house. We had taken him to our collective family heart.

Everyone wanted to talk to him, everyone did, everyone came away singing his praises, what a nice boy he was, how kind, thoughtful, talented. How lucky our groom was in having him as a friend.

Another round of sandwiches, another round of drinks, another round of songs. Popular Ronnie said, "Mary, you've got a great voice. Give us another."

"Me?" My mother beamed at him.

"Oh no. Not you. What's your name? Patsy, I mean. Aye, you."

I suppose he had got mixed up with all the Irish names. He turned to Patsy. She grinned and began to sing. My mother sat there trying to keep the beam from fading too quickly lest she give herself away. My dad gave her a weak, consoling smile. She clapped the loudest when Patsy finished.

I'll never forget her expression. She wasn't annoyed at his

thoughtlessness. She just felt embarrassed by her own foolishness.

Fancy being silly enough to think anyone would ask her to sing.

Relative Sanity

I was an orphan. Well, I still am really. You can't unbecome one, not unless you manage to revive your already dead parents. So there we have it. Orphaned at an early age and brought up by Aunt Emelda. She was bonkers. Now I know that that word, nowadays, has certain connotations; sexual inferences have attached themselves to it. Against its better judgement and outwith its control, no doubt, but attached they are and will remain for as long as the tabloid journalists, who coined it in the first place, can't come up with anything handier to stick in a headline. I cannot be held responsible for the serpentine workings of the language, or indeed the snake-like workings of the minds of certain members of the public. It's nothing to do with me so I ignore it and maintain that Emelda was bonkers.

Gays, that's another one. It's ridiculous to assume a whole section of the population adopt a certain mood because of their sexual predilections AND if they do why the hell should it be gay? Why not sombres? Why not have whole sections called Indifferents? Moroses? Calms?

That's the great advantage of Latin. With dead languages you know where you are. Words don't suddenly jump out of one meaning and into another. Same as dead parents, really. Now with live people and languages you're lost.

Emelda – I don't call her Aunt Emelda there are too many vowels at the beginning. It should really be Naunt Emelda, that would make it easier like an-aunt, or in French, tante – that would be OK too. But we're not French, so Emelda it is. Anyone who objects may sue. Although that sounds like somebody out of the Waltons or the Beverly Hill Billies. May Sue Clampet.

Anyway. Bonkers, she brought me up. Parents you can hate. Parents need to bring you up. It's their job. Oh yes, you can object, hate what they did, violently disagree with how they did it but you have to accept that they conceived you, begat you and all that shit. But if they have the bad grace to die on you and leave you in the hands of a decrepit old witch, what can you do?

It's normal, natural, almost bloody obligatory, to rebel against your parents, hate them, want to murder them. But how do you deal with an eccentric old busybody who, from the goodness of her heart, and through no moral necessity at all, takes you in and dedicates the rest of her spinstery old life to you. By God, it's hard.

I often think that all the stupid things she did – like refuse to tell me about Santa Claus in case it frightened me, or not let me have pets in case they died on me and left me grief-stricken, and any number of other crazy things – was because she had no instinct. Maybe a certain type of intelligence comes out with the afterbirth. Not the type of intelligence you need to understand the theory of relativity but the kind you need to be a kind relative. Or to keep your children relatively sane.

Maybe she had no instinct at all, maybe she just never thought. Oh, she theorised. She theorised all the bloody time. She just never bloody thought. She had a theory that too many people push their children to achieve academic success and this results in them having nervous breakdowns and committing suicide. To prevent this eventuality, she positively discouraged me from achieving results that were even average. How could I dare do anything other than impersonate the village idiot – not that we lived in a village – without it reflecting on and – possibly – giving people the impression that she was, in fact, shoving me down the road to academia. No, there was nothing else for it but to feign total numptosity.

It was hard at first, disguising the fact that I was a damn sight smarter than those stupid teachers. I kept wanting to show them how small and petty they were but for the sake of appearances I maintained a gormless persona.

Playing outside with other children? Oh no, not for me. I might get germs, or kidnapped.

Have you ever been deposited, on your first day at school, in a room with forty other children when you have never associated with children before? Not a pleasant experience. She used to come to the school at playtime and stand at the gate watching me. Wasn't that good and self-sacrificing of her?

She was a martyr. Gave up her career to look after me. Then made a career of telling people in front of me what she could have done if she had not had to give up her job.

She would never have had children of her own. Too much responsibility. Most people didn't, apparently, have a clue as to how to bring up children. It should be done by professionals.

All these theories would be pontificated upon to the assembled gathering.

She was an example of how parenting should be done. She dedicated her life to it. Attention, that's what children need. Most parents don't give them enough. They buy them toys and sweeties but what children really want is their parents' attention. I always got enough attention, she would let everyone know. Enough! I couldn't turn round without her being there. She wouldn't let me walk the length of myself. It was a vicious circle, she did everything for me so I never got the chance to do anything for myself, so I couldn't. I never got the experience. No practice. The more she did the less confident I became that I could do anything at all. On the odd occasions of rebellion when I would insist on doing something myself I would make a hash of it. She would step in. Smug old hag. Shaking her head and murmuring about where I would be without her.

A damn sight better off but she didn't realise that. She never ever did realise how much I resented her. Even at the very end.

I wonder if she smelt the paraffin. Did she ask herself how I got it. I didn't have a paraffin heater in my room any more but I don't think that the man in the newsagent's knew that.

If she were here she would have a theory about that as well. The newsagent would be classed most irresponsible for selling dangerous stuff like that to a child. Children could harm themselves with paraffin. If she were a shopkeeper she would never sell children dangerous substances. Cigarettes are another thing she would never sell to children if she had a shop. Matches too.

I like to think it was a fitting end. All the best martyrs are burned, after all. And witches. So now I'm re-orphaned, but that's OK. I quite like this place. People ignore you. I can sit here all day just looking out of the window and not a soul comes in.

Nice to be Nice

Anybody sitting here?
  No.
  Do you mind?
  No.
  Record, eh?
  Yes.
  I like the Record myself. Better than the Herald. Hate the
Herald.
  Uh hu.
  Always get the Record. Do you as well? Do you always get
the Record, same as me? Something in common, eh?
  I usually get the Herald but they were sold out.
  Ah. I quite like the Herald. When I said ... you know. I
didn't mean HATE the Herald. Nae offence, pal, eh? Nae
offence.
  Do you want to look at the paper?
  Naw. It's nice to be nice, that's all. Nice to be nice. That's
my motto. Ask anybody. Nice to be nice. Everybody knows
me.
  Very nice. (Going back to paper)
  Sorry, I'll shut up. Leave you in peace.
  Hmm.
  I know some people like to be left in peace. I'm like that
myself. Nothing worse, eh?
  Hm.
  Nice gaff, eh?
  Sorry?
  This place. This bar. Nice, eh?

Not bad.

Been in before? Know the place, do you?

A few times.

My local. Everybody knows me. Never out the place.

Really!

Good beer. Ever tried the heavy. Nice stuff. You should try it. Go on. Try it. Go on.

Maybe some other time.

It's good. You'll like it.

Look!

Not that I'm telling you what to drink. Naw. Just advice.

Hmm.

Funny, I've never seen you in here before.

No.

Usually just stay for the one, do you? Just the one is it, every time?

Sometimes. Sometimes not. Depends.

Depends? Depends on what?

Just depends.

Like whether or not she lets you off the lead. Eh?

Look pal ...

Sorry, sorry, mind my own business eh? Sorry.

Hmm.

It's just that sometimes you know. Women. You know. What's she like, a bit of a nag is she?

Can you drop it pal, eh?

Me and my big mouth, eh? Hit a raw nerve, eh?

No. Just drop it.

Nice to be ...

Drop it. OK.